My Uncle Rob

Steve Sandler

Illustrated by
Rob Cunningham

Washington Publishers
Tallahassee, Florida

My Uncle Rob

Text and Illustrations Copyright © 2008 Washington Publishers
Published by Washington Publishers SAN: 2542366
All rights reserved.

Washington Publishers
P.O. Box 12517
Tallahassee, Florida 32317

Steve Sandler
Rob Cunningham
My Uncle Rob
ISBN 978-0-9715721-5-7

Summary: When a young restaurant owner is stricken with Parkinson's disease his fate changes in more ways than one--he becomes an artist.

This book has been cataloged by the Library of Congress

PRINTED IN THE UNITED STATES OF AMERICA

10 9 8 7 6 5 4 3 2 1

Edited, printed and published in the USA
First edition: January 2008

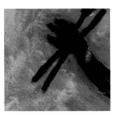 # Dedication

My Uncle Rob is dedicated to all of those who are challenged by Parkinson's Disease, their heroic caregivers, the physicians who treat them, and the tireless scientists who search for the ultimate cure.

This is my Uncle Rob standing in front of his restaurant, The Uptown Café. It was a cool place. People loved the great food and Uncle Rob's funny ways. I would stop by the café every day after school.

We had a deal. I would vacuum the dining room floor and Uncle Rob would feed me a sandwich or some delicious homemade soup, if there was any left. I always saved room for a slice of Uncle Rob's extra good banana nut bread.

When Uncle Rob was completely healthy he was a great frisbee player. . . twisting around. . . catching it behind his back. . . leaping high and snatching it between his legs!

Life was good.

One day Uncle Rob's life began to change forever. We were at the café chomping a tasty snack when I noticed Uncle Rob's right hand begin to shake.

It was weird but kind of funny.

Two days later it was still shaking. It wasn't really funny anymore.

Soon, the shaky hand was joined by a shaking foot. The foot dragged when he walked.

Then his old smile went crooked and disappeared.

His writing became so small that the café cooks could not read the orders he wrote down.

It was scary having so many weird things happen to someone I loved.

Uncle Rob was scared too. He went to see a Neurologist. A Neurologist is a brain doctor.

The Neurologist examined Uncle Rob. He made him walk back and forth on his heels and then his toes. He asked him to close his eyes and touch a finger to his nose. He asked him to put his hands in his lap and flip them over and back as fast as he could.

The doctor watched carefully and thought for a minute. He gently told Uncle Rob that he had Parkinson 's disease. The good news was there were medicines that could stop most

of the weird things from happening. The medicines work best when you live a simple, easygoing life. He said that soon Uncle Rob would want to sell the café. He should do something less stressful. This made Uncle Rob sad. He loved the café. But he knew the doctor was right. The café was already beginning to wear him out.

This is the day Uncle Rob sold the café. His workers threw him a surprise party. His regular customers came to thank him and wish him well. There were hugs and kisses everywhere.

I've never seen so much laughing and crying at the same time.

School had let out for the summer. Uncle Rob knew I'd been upset about his health. He said he had a present for me and gave me an envelope. Inside was an airplane ticket and a little book about a summer camp in the mountains of North Carolina. Hiking, rafting, meeting kids from all over. . .it would be the best summer ever!

When I got home from camp I ran straight to Uncle Rob's house to thank him. Uncle Rob opened the door wearing a huge old shirt. The sleeves were all rolled crooked. The shirt was splotched with bright paint like he'd been playing paintball and lost bad. His walls were covered with paintings. They were brightly colored, but strange. Some were faces of people. Others were of bizarre animals. There were several of villages with crooked buildings... more paintings than I could count.

Uncle Rob laughed so hard at my reaction that he almost fell over. He said I looked weirder than his paintings, kind of scared and curious and amused all at the same time. Uncle Rob explained that he had always wanted to be an artist but never had the time. Painting had become the best medicine for Parkinson's.

Uncle Rob had studied a bunch of famous painters' work by reading books he'd gotten from the library. He learned a method called "No Fear Painting" which encouraged him to use colors and shapes that did not match the colors and shapes of the people and things he painted.

"If I wanted my paintings to look exactly like the real thing I'd use a camera," said Uncle Rob.

Uncle Rob's paintings that I like best: This man's skin is not the color of any real person I know. Uncle Rob says that color tells about emotions and feelings.

This lady's greenish skin makes me think she is tired.

This picture has Uncle Rob right in the middle of it, painting a picture of the countryside. I could romp and climb trees all day in a place like that.

This is a cityscape. Uncle Rob says it's not anyplace he's really been, but in his mind he spent a week there last May. He said the food was terrific, but it rained the whole time he was there. I punched him in the arm for saying something so silly.

Uncle Rob paints lots of goofy animals...

funny goats, cats, and birds.

But horses are his favorite animal to paint. When he was my age, he helped a friend herd cows on the weekends.   He says he's had a soft spot for horses ever since then...especially blue and green horses. Uncle Rob is a hoot!

Uncle Rob's favorite paintings are ones he calls abstracts. He breaks all the rules of the real world in these paintings. Animals float in the air. People have trees growing out of their heads. Anything goes!

Some critters he paints are a combination of three or four different animals.

I ask him what he is trying to say with these abstract paintings. He says he'll never tell and I'd be better off trying to think of what the pictures mean to me. I told him they mean that he's a bull goose loony. We both laughed so hard we had to sit down.

Uncle Rob is right. Good art should make you think.

So I thought. . .

Fifteen years have passed since the day Uncle Rob's hand began to shake. While his Parkinson's disease has slowly gotten worse, the medicines that help him have gotten better. Life is hard but he's doing fine. He paints every day and sells his paintings in galleries all over the country. That's pretty amazing for a guy whose hand shakes when he paints and who never drew anything until he was nearly 50.

After thinking about all of Uncle Rob's paintings, this is my favorite.

The clown is Uncle Rob and the bull is the Parkinson's Disease.

Uncle Rob faces the sharp, pointy-horned bull with bravery and a courageous smile.

I've learned from Uncle Rob that no matter how your life turns, if you face each day with courage and a smile, you can do anything!

Steve Sandler (left) is an author, and a former teacher of the deaf, the blind, and preschool computer educator. He was diagnosed with Parkinson's disease in 1999. He resides in Tallahassee Florida.

Rob Cunningham was a restaurateur until Parkinson's disease changed his life. Now, he paints full time. He has sold his work nationwide and is the subject of a film documentary called "Painting on Parkinson's". Rob lives in Tallahassee near his best friend, Steve.

For more information about Parkinson's disease contact the following organizations:

National Parkinson's Foundation, Inc.
www.parkinson.org
1501 N.W. 9th Avenue / Bob Hope Road
Miami, Florida 33136-1494
(800) 327-4545

American Parkinson's Disease Association
ww.apdaparkinson.org
135 Parkinson Avenue
Staten Island, NY 10305
(800) 223-2732

Parkinson's Disease Foundation
www.pdf.org
1359 Broadway, Suite 1509
New York, NY 10018
(800) 457-6676

The Parkinson Alliance
www.parkinsonalliance.org
Post Office Box 308
Kingston, New Jersey 08528-0308
(800) 579-8440

Parkinson's Action Network
www.parkinsonsaction.org
1025 Vermont Ave, NW Suite 1120
Washington, DC 20005
(800) 850-4726

The Michael J. Fox Foundation for Parkinson's Research
www.michaeljfox.org
Church Street Station
P.O. Box 780
New York, NY 10008-0780
(800) 327-4545

Other books by

Washington Publishers

<u>Baby Girl or Baby Boy</u>
Mark Moore, M.D. and Lisa Moore, RN

"Baby Girl or Baby Boy" is written by a Doctor and a Nurse and
contains the medical knowledge couples need to know on natural
gender selection techniques—a "how to" manual on
how to make a baby girl or baby boy.

<u>Forever Mom</u>
Kelly Ashey

In a world turned upside-down, her biggest sorrow was not
the loss of her own life, but the thought that she might not be
there for her children--to love them, guide them and
care for them as they grew up.
Kelly wanted to be their "Forever Mom".

These books are available at your local bookseller
or online @ amazon.com

Learn more @ www.washingtonpublishers.com